Dark Poetry

by Fenris Mau

Knowing

when I Fall

the Wind will caress me

so I am not Lost

the trees will sing my name

until Winter

then their crooked arms

will reach up

touch the silver Eye

and show

how strong my Spirit was

so when the wind

lets Go

I have known Peace

The Tree and the Raven

Writhing

the black tree sways

Alone

Old its days

a limb

stretching hindered

pointing north

holds its kindred

A raven

poised still

wings outstretched

elegant Kill

Sleek his face

hard his expression

his ways are sure

he knows no confession

Bold

he calls

yet reticent

the Tree

they speak for each other

in Song

and Flee

Desperate

the Tree

reaches out

and Cries

waiting

for years

and finally

Dies

Leaving

I could smile

find Joy

feel good

Inside

with you

so warm

nothing

to Hide

say it again

say you don't Know

whether to Die

or let it Grow

Regretting my life

on the edge Dying

just Holding tight

not even crying

I would smile

but my face was torn

I have no emotion

just loss and Forlorn

me

alone

so cold

my Fate

took

the Love

and Burned it

Hate

caress me still

get blood on your shirt

this life was a waste

all I did was Hurt

take my Leave

everything's alright

I wasn't meant to be here

I'm not going to fight

Let me Go

Us

there is Silence

but I still hear your voice

you're still there waiting

but our Pain was our choice

alone I am Lost

my life is Yours

what started the grief

the inner wars?

my home is

where You are

almost there

not too far

then we Live

above the Lost

Forget the Pain

the Lives we cost

how many times

do we keep giving in

turning around

and calling it sin

yet in the end

we built the trust

the only One

we need is Us

Tried to Tell you

but it's too late

thought this was yours

but it's Our fate

Living Again

talons

long enough

to pierce the Heart

takes the Life

and rips apart

eyes hollowed

black and dull

Bloody Lies

drip down

the skull

covers the face

with gray brittle hair

makes us forget

the times that Weren't there

against the wall

pinning us Helpless

bites our throats

we know we can't stop this

stealing our breath

a Knife in our hands

drop it cold

it's going as Planned

sliding down

stain the wall

No One there

to break our fall

choking bitter

suffer hard

living again

yet this time Scarred

Remember

remembering Things

I wish I'd forget

fill me with sorrow

Hate and Regret

love always

Cut it Off

harden my Heart

make me soft

truth or lies

words you speak

make me Strong

make me Weak

piece me together

split me in half

heal and destroy

cry and laugh

Love Kills

follows me Close

sick on a high

a Lethal dose

Self

Darkness surrounds me

deep | Inhale

I try to resist

the Shadows prevail

a constant wound

never healed

a burden to life with

a fate sealed

the voice inside

I cannot ignore

I try to reverse it

it cries for More

tear myself open

try to let it free

but this can't be altered

this is Me

a dream

that comes and passes

always fading

never clear

might as well forget me now

I

was never here

Trapped

wretched claws

grow

from my grave

everything broken

cannot be saved

chained

deep to the roots

of the grim earth

cannot be saved

chained

deep to the roots

of the grim earth

as my dry

crooked face

reaches the surface

takes a breath

one last time

looks up

the Sky

a suffocated cage

light sharply peers

cracking my skin

I am Trapped

disown my Within

I once Loved

the Moon

thought it was Free

but as I turn

to crumbling dust

I know now

it is as helpless

as Controlled

as me

Masks

the Scars are seen

but do they really care

only One

just One

some pretend

and they wear

masks on their face

but does that one know

do they know what it is in the mind?

the words you see that make

you Blind

takes your breath and makes

you gasp
steal it
it's all you had
forever staring
what does it do to them?
they Forget

Slowing

everyone's heart

is beating

some slower than others

signifying closeness

to Death

but sometimes

the ones beating

the fastest

want it to stop

blood flows

isolated alone

friends laugh beside me

no concern is shown

let the demon

steal my Life

tear up my world

with the Knife

never safe

never secure

without Death

never a Cure

try to change my mind

too late

too behind

I can't be blamed for This

you're Blind

might as well

do it Now

while I Know

Exactly how

the dwindling sound

that everyone ignores

my heart

is beating faster than yours

Gone

when the Moon

has Risen high

when I have Awaken

Mourn and Fly

when you stopped

to make me Bend

made my scars Deeper

Darker trend

your Words burn

I try to Live

emotion has left

no more to give

stand noble

violent the war

here alone | suffer

| reach for the gun once more

when the sun Falls

when your spirit dies

when the sky has faded

so have |

Broken

sitting in the corner

shaking

can you hear my heart

beating

breaking

blood sheds to the cold floor

fear seeps in deeply

to the core

I watch you pass me

love and hate stir within

I close my eyes

you can't see this Sin

I chase

this dismay

never knew

it would turn this way

thought I knew but it's all just a fake

I'm not like you

this is why

I'm Awake

Flooded Between

the last Strike

pulls me Below

already can't breathe

hunger and sleep depart

without looking back

I don't even miss it

because all that's on my mind

is you

but your eyes

turn Grey

like the mist

that has flooded between us

each day

you grow deaf

as the soil

eats at my dying flesh

don't have long

Escape

even in

my Last breath

I can smile

because they

are not there

but I am not alone

this is home

when the moon grows old

and my tired heart slows

when I Fall

down cold to the snow

blood stains my fur

streams down my tongue

teases all the howls past sung

eyes shine dark like moons

they stare

drifting away

I am here to Stay

no walls to confine me

blind me

now I am Free

Forgotten Night

blank eyes

face the sky

seeing nothing

never cry

moon shines cold

on my body painted red

forget what's left behind me

I'll never know I'm dead

I disappeared

miss you like hell

don't know what happened

the night I Fell

you don't care

it's not my concern

sadness or anger

try to discern

blank eyes

face the sky

seeing nothing

never cry

Last

laying here slain

I reminisce with the still

never forget the past

the kills

I watched it drain

my life from within

tried to numb

the strife and the sin

tried to show me Fear

and I fled

scarred my mind

you so slyly fed

every night

I told myself it'd be over soon

taught me to fight

and turn against the Moon

fills the dread and makes it Die

the knife will speak and answer why

then

for one second

my last breath

makes you see

Promise

growl in Your ear

let you know

I'm still Here

bite at your face

bring you Down

you're a waste

make us the same

as the crows

chant our name

"Silenced

we've stared at you

solemn

long past

now it is you

after all your oaths cast"

shivering Frozen

alone and in pain

birds above circle

cry

makes it rain

darkening silence

closing in red

forget what I lost

the Promise you said

Away

I cannot

find freedom

within the walls

that's why I Fall

why can't the moon

warm my resting place

guide my way

then I would stay

the trees speak to me Truths

around them I have flown

I

am not alone

the wind

answers to me strength

to endure

tear at my soul

and make my heart black

you are the one that makes me

bite back

call me dead

heartless

call me violent

this is why

I stay so silent

Alone

Stone is your Speak

I watch your face

your mind is closed

words with tears traces

you were the dark shadow

scarcely ever seen

the blackest nightmare

coiled in my dreams

watched my own life

leave

fallen yet sacred

hiding

deceives me

but I can still find peace

when I look through

my kindred's eyes

we cease

but I am not here

just watching

as the darkness

closes in

Slain

I can't cry anymore

is it me?

after all the nights

my tears would bleed?

I can't die anymore

is it you?

showed me living hell

I don't know what to do

hanging by a thread

cut it and I'm dead

I've already been killed

apparently it's my will

yelling in agony screaming in pain

fall to the ground

I'm finally slain

Faceless

emotionless Tears

fall upon my knees

dead to my cries

all my earnest pleas

lay out my carcass

for all to see me dull

humiliate my honor

and curse upon my skull

tell me I deserve to die

and in your mind recite

as I begin to suffocate

and lie that it's alright

lay me down

make me drown
touch my hair
wind makes it dance

wonder why I look so faceless

when you put me in this trance

To Protect

looking Down

I see the Blade

stabbed deep

into my souled

I won't look up

but I know

the blade is yours

mine disguised

an ominous weapon

of destruction

is actually a shield

lowered

even if

you twist the blade

my weapon

will not arise

my blood cries

for the battle

but my heart

sings in shame

now who is greater

as I

am forgotten

Flight

I watch you

from Darkness I stare

as you dance in your bliss

and praise the masks that you wear

I watch you sink

the river mirrors our deaths

nothing to hope for

nothing to protect

our shadows choke us

voices echo in our mind

how can you let me die like this

I never led you blind

the graceful dance of Death

the Kiss that turns to Bite

baited to the kill

leaves me dead and takes to flight

feel the rhythm

your heart beating in your head

drown in our tears

your blood turns cold

black and red

still and barren

our silent bones regret

while we were forever here

you never Killed us yet

Waiting

got me to Smile

but I'm Fading away

you know what to do

to save my life

so I lie in wait

my knives are not bared

only defending myself

silently

until that shadow disappears

until then

my way is lost

my senses numbed

the thought begs

that this is my fate

disarm yourself

and cleanse your soul

I am Waiting

Cursed

I try to come awake

try to make myself feel

but then I'm just reminded

this is all real

one more acquaintance

another thing to lose

isn't that all we do

live short and get used

turn from truth

confessions I pour into your hands

blown away simply

Endless desert sands

seize the life

ignore the pain

deaf to the cries

no longer sane

now I'm safe

nothing they can do

nothing to make

this fate come true

escape this world

not a soul to tell

alone yet surrounded

we Curse ourselves

Fate

remember the Lies

steal the past

kill my spirit

make it last

throw me down

I don't care

a thousand scars

my heart will bare

kiss a bullet

embrace a flame

whatever it takes

forget my name

stare me down
watch me bleed
condemn the truth

yet on it feed

who can stop

these bloody hands

flooded with guilt

none understand

think about it

once more

maybe nine

countless times

I've almost died

feign security

confidence

no concern

as my Sight

will fall black

and my soul

will burn

dying from

this double fate

one of love

and one of hate

Here

still envision the Past

the Terrors it brought

the grasp for Life

and then it was shot

the moon, a talon

grips me no more

finally surfaced

so silent the shore

parallel to the sky

my blanket is the waves

I whisper the question

What kills and what saves?

my eyes are closed

the answer is Clear

let the shadow wane

you're never here

Wait for me

I'll be there

stay with me

I don't care

waiting for you

you'll be there

ill stay with you

do you care?

Killing

I see the truth

dripping

from your empty eyes

 as you watch me

hunger and cold

tell me lies

inner feelings voices in my mind fight

you've no idea

what I'd do to make it right

desperate cries

fears come awake

never forgetting

the lives you take

the eager flame

burns in my mind

never dies out

I can't Leave this behind

moon reflects

upon my bones

wind

carries away

my lonesome moans

the bite that kills

the gaze blood spills

dying powers

last few hours

forget me

and I'll forget you

but remember the day

you killed me too

Drowning

the liquid Bullet

sinks in deep

steals the mind

you tried to keep

slowly shot down

until your final fall

but I can't tell you

you know it all

hypnotized

it blinds your eyes

makes no sense

whispers lies

is it the venom

that rids of your fears

or the cup of blood

that catches your tears?

drink it all

have your night

drown alone

let it bite

watch me suffer

blame me for it too

make me the one that dies

long before you do

Stolen

Memories of the past

the sharpness is sly

we share the moon alone

and smile as we die

the hunt was ours

you ran beside me

but I have escaped

now you must find me

solemn is our gaze

our lives forsaken

follow my path

before you are taken

every time I come Alive

close my eyes

the wind is your fur

can't remember the darkened blur

Howls drowned silent

pain stabbing deep

found the way to make us bite

and stolen what we Keep

The Bird

why is it

we come and go

so easily

like a game

like a bird

beautiful its song

though it may kill

none notice

none care

to know

apparent innocence

is deadly

indeed

Home

after the apocalypse

how can you

still yet melt

around my soul

the wax that burns

and holds me down

as it becomes colder

that my heart has ever seen

your embrace

covers my eyes

which no longer seek

disables my arms

that no longer grasp

muffles my heart

which never cries out again

I cannot

warm enough to move

but why would I ever want to again?

this home encases me

so I will not fall

but how can I fall when I can't get up?

My Demons

heart of a saint

soul of a sinner

the secrets are locked

deep inside

your cavern of fate

I approached with a dagger

and you bit at my throat

now I return

with gifts

my eyes

are even closed

every mystery you lock away

leaves a growing scar

yet I keep walking

if you let me in

our pain will be shared

but not cleave us apart

I am vulnerable

speak well and quickly

for my time

here is short

and my cavern possessed

all the same

the demons that haunt you

now make me

their prey

as I crumble

Untitled

I'm dying

but how could you know

you will never

know my pain

no one ever has

and yet why

do I bother to write

Stay

lays the scream

beside the bed

hides the joke

you threw and fled

rips the care

and fakes it strong

turned and smiled

forgot it's wrong

not behind us yet

live it while it lasts

soon it will be dead for us

a dream of living past

silent all stare

reflect the lies told

blind we see

not the moon grow old

black are the eyes

that stab us through

ice is the breath

that bites too soon

scars of defeat crawl up my arms

ignored it all

the poison that harms

bitter it stings

endless the thought

kills the hope

we've tirelessly sought

hears nothing move

watch it die slow

revealed the secrets

we tried to show

again it's gone

alone is the prey

but never expected

I want it to stay

Spoken

Memories lost

at gun point cornered

slowly

give in

close my eyes

every painful word

I chase you

watch you chase me

I'm standing right beside you

the spirit you can't see

no one

run from the other

choose which Side

Prey or Brother

emotions grow numb

hope lingers over my shoulders

scarcely there

grows even colder

my hopes

have teased me

faded away

crushed me

pretended to stay

soft | whisper

in pain you hear

the speak of agony

drawing near

now they can

understand

killed by the bite

subconsciously planned

Silent Voices

close your eyes

hear my howl

feel your pulse

faster

faster

my voice

keeps calling

goes unanswered

I'm falling

falling

I can hear your nervous heart beating

try to run

this is cheating

cheating

watch my eyes

silent stare

hear my footsteps

closer

closer

look around

feel the night

watch the moon

guide my bite

take a chance

call my name

but can't you see

I'm Not the Same

forget the past

forget the lies

fill the trees

with your cries

your voice

keeps calling

goes unanswered

you're falling

falling

close your eyes

hear my growl

feel your pulse

slower

slower

The Enemy

the Accusations

you throw

keep me tied

to the floor

is it me?

my blood cries out

but stays within

sealed by promise

I grasp for words

nothing makes

my speak gain wisdom

escape the shadows

I glimpsed

before you closed the door

if I try

to speak with them

your claws unsheathe

to protect

if I ask you

of my visions

your bitter words

poison

what I last spoke

I must be

the Enemy

Overtaken

killing time

you keep

your demons close

my last hours near

as your grey eyes

turn black

and my breath

is stilled

if my soul

was drowned in sin

stained with blood

of self hatred

would my place be filled

with the embrace

of your demon?

the mist of my life

is now drifting

into the reflection

of the moon

I am

but a shadow now

my place has already been overtaken

the seal of refraining

from silence

has been obeyed

yet still

I am being slain

powerless

the shadows now bring my comfort

Haste

enjoy the look

of my blind eyes

that dilate

when I fade

because my expression

when I am conscious

becomes your hatred

I close them

hoping

your grip will soften

but I can only know

if you have

by taking another glimpse

I feel nothing

my blood stops

and runs even colder

kill me already

let it be Over

Silver Sky

my Field has shadows

no sun

no moon

my dance Has sin

just endless gloom

my bones will reveal

my skin's just a map

the silent cries

that filled all the gaps

wash your shore

on my formless eclipse your sun

behind your moon

split in half

Turning

hand runs softly

down my face

love was there

just a waste

silent I wait

still and alone

exchanging secrets

with dying bones

stabbed with hate

this is my fate

return the curse

but it's too late

twist the sword

in your heart stabbed through

share the misery

that I had too

smile once more

make it last

you don't exist

nor does the past

Never

sharing souls

intriguing indeed

slice it off

watch it bleed

small immortals

in my veins

worth the life

the endless pains

say the words

don't say a thing

steal away my spirit

and lie about a ring

forever I remain

barren and keen

trust beyond belief

no longer will I lean

your heart is mine

I'd kill for you

go the hell away

I'm dying for you

I'll never come back

Daring

Every second

rakes my body

into the earth

my flames

have lost their warmth

but still consume

what's left of my bones

still able

to turn my head

I look at you

daring to look

upon your face

only to see

you are turned

the other way

Further

silently

my past

swallows me whole

as the remains of my iris

see you hiding

there are no words

I dare grasp

else I be forgotten

and trodden down

to nothing more

than the thought

of a secluded secret

that has always

been out of my reach

trying to make us whole

I begged answers

which could only reap

my sorrowful fate

as I had feared so

your guarding demons

spread out further

so none can get close

I am already nearly out of sight

my figure is a mere shadow

a silhouette

of a free spirit

that entrapped its own soul

for the sake of the false God

of wisdom

Solace

Alas, solace within

the mirror serene

yet the reflection

obstructs the other

angel and demon

who am I to join

this purity

that has never been mine?

Keeping

This is to the heart

I never had

the one that never hurt

was silver clad

so to this I bid

my soul away

hope to rid

of their dismay

I drink the fruit

that makes me sleep

memories harden

a bitter Keep

CPSIA information can be obtained
at www.ICGtesting.com
Printed in the USA
LVHW081545270920
667211LV00020B/2807